Bob and Larry's
CLUES TO GOOD NEWS

INTEGRITY®
PUBLISHERS
family

www.bigidea.com

www.integritypublishers.com

Bob and Larry's Clues to Good News

ISBN: 1-591-45255-4

Copyright © 2005 by Big Idea, Inc.

Illustrations copyright © 2005 by Big Idea, Inc.

Requests for information should be addressed to:

Integrity Publishers

5250 Virginia Way, Suite 110

Brentwood, TN 37027

Written by: Cindy Kenney

Illustrated by: Greg Hardin

Bob and Larry's
CLUES TO
GOOD NEWS

By Cindy Kenney

Illustrated by Greg Hardin

"Indiana Larry!"

"Larry, that's not your name."

"Shhhh! Dakota Bob, we have gone undercover."

"Dakota who? We don't have to go undercover, Larry. We're just helping the kids find some clues."

"Oh! A secret mission."

"Not really, Larry. We're going to help kids find answers to their questions about God."

"Oh! I get it! It's a treasure hunt!"

"Well, yeah! Because God is the best treasure of all!"

"Then I'm ready, Bob. Let's go on a treasure hunt!"

"Hey Kids! You're invited to go on this treasure hunt with us. Just find the clues to the Good News and collect the answers that will lead YOU to the treasure!"

"We're going to visit some of our favorite Veggie places to look for clues. Let's start by visiting Qwerty to search for Clue #1."

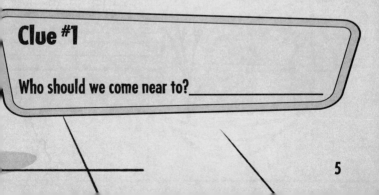

Clue #1

Who should we come near to?_____

6

"Look! Qwerty has our first clue! It's from the Bible, and it says, *'Come near to God and he will come near to you.'* James 4:8. That's the place where you can find it in the Bible."

"Got it, Bob. When we've got questions for God, he wants us to go to him for the answers!"

"Right, Larry! So the answer to Clue #1 is **GOD**."

"This is right up my alley, Bob."

"Okay, Larry, but don't get out your bowling shoes yet. We've got some other clues to find, first. Next stop, the Veggie Lagoon!"

"Swimming! Snorkeling! Building sand castles. Getting a tan. Whoopee! I can't wait!"

Who is God?

Grab your beach towel and head to the Veggie Lagoon with Bob and Larry to discover the answer to this question and find the next clue to the puzzle:

God created everything in the _____.

"Last one there is a cross-eyed snail!"

"Hey, Bob! I've been hiking, swimming, snorkeling, and fishing. I still can't find the next clue or the answer to the question: Who is God?"

"Well gee, Larry, I have found the catch of the day!"

"I've got a nibble. It's a BIG one! I can't…seem to…pull…it out…of the waaaaaaater! Yikes!"

"Are you okay, Larry?"

"A-okay Bob! And look what I caught—an anchor with an old shoe hooked onto it. That's no help. We don't even wear shoes."

"But look at the anchor, Larry! It says something on it."

"'In the beginning God created the heavens and the earth.' Genesis 1:1. That's it Bob! That's the answer!"

"It sure is, Larry! That's what it says right here in my Bible. It's the very first sentence of the book. The Bible is the anchor to all our questions!"

"It also has the answer to Clue #2. God created everything in the **WORLD**. Looks like we've caught some good news!"

Who is God?

"In the beginning,
God created the
heavens and
the earth."
Genesis 1:1

Bob the Tomato
and Larry the Cucumber
have good news to report from the Veggie
Lagoon. They found the answer to the
question: Who is God?

God is our Creator. God made the
land and the sea. He created everything in
the whole world! God made the grass and
trees, flowers and fruit. God created every
animal, bird, and fish.

"And my rubber ducky!" adds ace
reporter, Larry the Cucumber. "God even

created those pesky flies and mosquitoes that gave me lots of itchy bumps last summer. The good news is that God also made me all better!"

After God created our beautiful world and everything in it, God created people—and guess what kids! God created **YOU**.

Why did God do all that? God created us so that he can have a family. God is our Father. God is our Friend. And most of all, God wants to have a wonderful, awesome relationship with YOU. God wants to connect with you every day, because he loves you!

You can read more about it in the Bible.

Five-Day Forecast for Veggie Lagoon

Hi 85° Lo 68°
Every Day!

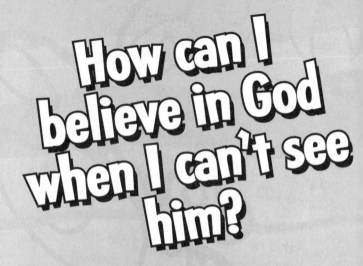

How can I believe in God when I can't see him?

Don't forget your suntan lotion when you head back to the Veggie Lagoon to help Bob and Larry find the answer to this question and the next clue:

Clue #3

Faith means we can _____ in something we can't see.

"Last one there is a dizzy dolphin!"

"Hey, Bob! I found the treasure!"

"You found God?"

"No silly, but I did find a marshmallow fork…an old swim cap…a potato masher…a broken toaster…a hair dryer…"

"Ahhh, okay, Larry. I found something, too!"

"Just a minute, Bob. I also found a jack-in-the-box, and it just popped up with some good news!"

"Is it Hebrews 11:1 from the Bible?"

"Yep, and it tells all about faith. How did you know?"

"I had faith, Larry."

"So faith means we can believe in something that we can't see! That's the next clue! Let's go report it in the *VeggieConnections News*!"

"Super idea, Larry! It's great news to let others know that whoever **BELIEVES** in God is showing faith in him!"

How can I believe in God when I can't see him?

"Faith is being sure of what we hope for and certain of what we do not see."

Hebrews 11:1

Bob and Larry uncovered a buried treasure at the Veggie Lagoon and learned about faith.

Have you ever wondered how you can feel and hear the wind blow, but you can't see it? Even though we can't see the wind, we know it's there.

Faith in God is a little like that, too. Faith is all about believing in God—

even though we can't see him. We have to trust that God is real, based on what we know in our heart to be true.

We learn those things in the Bible, God's history book. It's filled with stories told by people who lived a long time ago, and it also tells us about the true story of a man named Jesus.

The Bible helps us to understand that faith in God is all about believing that God made you and has a special plan for your life.

Now that's good news you can believe in!

What happens when I trust God?

Mount your horses and ride off to Dodgeball City with Bob and Larry to find the answer to this question and the next clue:

God gives me joy and peace when I trust in _____.

"C'mon, Bob! Last one there is a snake with chicken pox!"

"I don't think snakes get chicken pox, Larry!"

"Lucky for you, then, because I'm way ahead of you!"

"Oh give me a clue, where the cows all go "moo,"
and the skies are not cloudy all day! Where seldom is
found, anything on the ground, and tomatoes don't
help anyway!"

"Larry, what kind of song is that?"

"That's Cowboy Larry to you, partner. Ready to hear my next verse?"

"I think we should get back to work."

♪♫ "Oh give me a break; it is all I can take! Don't make me keep working this way! I'm just having fun; we'll get our work done before the sun sets on this day!" ♪♫

"Larry, we aren't acting the way God wants us to."

"You're right, partner. I'm sorry."

"I'm sorry, too. Hey, cowboy, want to see something?"

"In just one yippee-ki-ay minute! Looky here! Good thing the horses didn't nibble on this. It's the next Good News clue!"

"From Romans 15:13?"

"Boy howdy, sure enough! It's all about peace and joy!"

"So we can have hope and don't have to worry when we trust in **HIM**."

"Let's git along partner—let's report what we found in the *VeggieConnections News*."

What happens when I trust God?

"May the God of hope fill you with all joy and peace as you trust in him, so that you may overflow with hope by the power of the Holy Spirit."
Romans 15:13

Despite some problems at the Which Way Corral in Dodgeball City, Bob and Larry forgave each other.

God knows that we all do things that are wrong. But if we ask him to forgive our sins and trust in him, he will forgiv us. God will fill us with joy and peace.

That's why God sent his Son, Jesus, to earth. God wanted to give us hope.

God knew that our sins would hurt our connection to him. So God sent his Son, Jesus, to take the punishment for our sins by dying on a cross—so that we can be forgiven! And our connection with God is forever healed.

That's how much God loves us—and that's how we know we can trust God with our lives.

Now that's good news you can trust!

Lost and Found

LOST: Acts of love in our family. If found, please return to any family member. Reward—hugs and smiles.

FOUND: Extra chores done in secret. If they were done by you, please accept our thanks!

Why did Jesus have to die?

Saddle up and ride off into the sunset with Bob and Larry to Dodgeball City one more time to find the answer to this question and the next clue:

Jesus died to forgive our sins and give us the gift of

_____ _____.

"Last one to the Which Way Corral is a horse with no tail!"

"Ouch! These tumbleweeds are prickly."

"Gotta dodge 'em, Larry."

"Then how am I supposed to round up the next clue?"

"Maybe the answers aren't in those tumbleweeds, partner."

"Then where are they?"

"Saddle up, and I'll tell ya!"

"Hold that thought, Bob! They don't call me Indiana Larry for nothing!"

"Larry! We don't call you Indiana Larry."

"Hold that thought, too, Bob! There's a cowboy hat caught in this tumbleweed. I think the next clue is inside the hat. It's from John 11:25-26."

"That's it! Jesus tells us that whoever believes in him will live, which gives us the answer to Clue # 5, **ETERNAL LIFE**. Good job Kentucky Larry!"

"Kentucky Larry?"

"Okay…Colorado Larry? Wyoming Larry? Arizona Larry?"

"Bob, why are you calling me those names?"

"I thought you wanted to be called by different names of the United States!"

"Why would you think that?"

"Not a clue, Larry."

"You're so silly, Bob. We're finding lots of clues! C'mon, cowboy! We've got to report it in the *VeggieConnections News* before sundown! Giddy-up!"

Why did Jesus have to die?

"I am the resurrection and the life. He who believes in me will live, even though he dies; and whoever lives and believes in me will never die."
John 11:25–26

Reporters Bob and Larry rode off to Dodgeball City with a really sad question: Why did Jesus have to die?

We don't always listen to God the way he wants us to. That's because we want to do things our own way instead of God's way. When we choose to do things that we know are wrong, that's called sin. When w sin, it breaks our connection with God. God brought Jesus into the world because he wants us to know more about him. God wants us to understand how much he loves us and that we need forgiveness from our sins. God misses having a connection with us when we do wrong.

Everyone sins. But no matter how hard we try, we can't fix our connection with God by ourselves.

So God sent his Son, Jesus, to show how much he loves us. Jesus died for our sins to take our punishment for doing wrong. Jesus died for us so that our sins could be forgiven and our connection with God forever repaired. After Jesus died, he rose from the dead and came back to earth for a very short time before going to live with God. He wanted to show us his promise of life forever will really happen!

That means if YOU believe in Jesus, YOU will have life forever in heaven with God, too!

That's good news you can live for!

How can I talk to God?

Check the time and see if it matches the clock tower at a little town called Snoodleburg. Join Bob and Larry as they head over to there to visit with the Snoodles—fun little folks who eat pancakes with noodles! See if you can figure out the answer to the next clue while you're there!

Clue #6

When you talk to God, you will find out how much you are

_____.

"Come out, come out wherever you are!"

"I'm right here, Larry."

"Bob, I'm playing hide-and-go seek with the Snoodles."

"Instead of looking for Snoodles, you should be looking for our next clue."

"I was hoping to find a Snoodle who would help me find it!"

"We don't need a Snoodle to show us where it is."

"Maybe a Snoodle bug, then"

"We don't need a Snoodle bug, either."

"How about a Snoodle bird?"

"Nope."

"A Snoodle bunny?"

"Larry, we don't need a Snoodle bug, bird, or bunny."

"How about a Snoodle cat, crab, or cow? Or a Snoodle snake, skunk, or sheep? "

"Larry, I've got the clue right here…"

"Ah! Maybe not a Snoodle toad, tiger, or tomato! But here it is, falling right out of the Snoodle tower. It says the next clue is in Matthew 7:7."

"That was a great Snoodle snag! Because Matthew 7:7 is all about how God's door is always open to us. It shows us how much we are **LOVED**, which is the answer to clue #6!"

"Let's tell the kids how they can talk to God in our next *VeggieConnections'* article!"

How can I talk to God?

"Ask and it will be given to you; seek and you will find; knock and the door will be opened to you."
Matthew 7:7

Bob and Larry found out that we can talk to God any time, any place! And when we talk to God, that's called prayer.

God loves us so much that he sent his Son, Jesus, so we can have a very personal relationship with him. That means when we believe in God's love and the forgiveness that Jesus gave us, God will come to live in our heart forever. That relationship will grow when we talk to God in prayer.

So all we have to do is ASK God, and he will provide for us. It doesn't matter where we are or what we're doing. God will listen to what we have to say.

All we need to do is SEEK God, and we will find him at work in our lives. God is our Creator, and he is everywhere! He wants us to keep looking to him for help, understanding, wisdom, and love.

All we need to do is KNOCK, and God will open the door to us through his Son, Jesus. God wants to be a part of our lives.

God wants us to ask, seek, and knock at his door every day. That's because God wants to connect to us so we can know him better.

Five-Day Forecast for Snoodleburg

Hi 72° Lo 72°

Every Day!

How does God want me to spend my time?

Don't be late when Bob and Larry head over to the Chocolate Factory to find the answer to this question and the next clue!

Clue #7

God wants us to put him first, so _____

_____us the Bible so we will grow in wisdom.

"C'mon, Bob! Last one to the Chocolate Factory is a vanilla bunny!"

"Larry! We're going to a chocolate factory…"

"One bunny, two bunnies, three bunnies, four. Five bunnies, six bunnies; clue's in the drawer!"

"Really, Larry? Did you find a clue in the drawer?"

"No, just hoping! Or is that hopping?"

"Larry, why don't you come over here a minute and look at what I found…"

"Seven bunnies, eight bunnies, nine bunnies, ten. Eleven bunnies, twelve bunnies, clue's under the hen!"

"There aren't any hens in the Chocolate Factory, Larry, just bunnies."

"But I've tried everything else, Bob. I'm punching out of the Chocolate Factory and calling it a day!"

"You don't have to do that, Larry…"

"You're right! Bob, I found the next clue right here on the time clock! It says to look at Psalm 90:12."

"Psalm 90 talks about how we should spend our time. In fact, God gave us the entire Bible so that we can gain wisdom and learn more about him."

"So everything **HE GAVE** us shows how much he loves us. I know how we should spend our time, Bob!"

"How?"

"By putting God first! Let's get to press and tell the kids what we learned!"

How does God want me to spend my time?

"Teach us to make the most of our time, so that we may grow in wisdom."

Psalm 90:12, NLT

The latest news from our *Veggie-Connections* reporters is that God wants us to spend our time wisely and put him first. But what does that mean?

Spending our time wisely means doing what is most important first. Every day is a gift from God who made each of us special and loves us very much! So we should put God first in our life.

Every day we have to make choices about

how to spend our time. God wants us to make the most of it! So after we decide what's most important to us, our choices should be a sign of that to others.

When we decide to put God first, we spend our time doing the things God wants us to do—and doing what's right!

God is with us all the time, and God wants us to spend our time with him, too. That means making time to talk to God, worship God, and learn from God by reading his Word in the Bible.

God wants us to trust in his timing. Only God can see the big picture of the entire world and what's going to happen. So when we don't get what we want when we talk to God, we still have to trust in him.

Remember: God made you special and he loves you very much!

What are the things God wants me to do?

Hop on over to the assembly line with Bob and Larry as they return to the Chocolate Factory to find the answer to this question and the next clue!

Clue #8

_____ wants to know what God wants them to do should turn to the two most important commands that Jesus gave.

"The last one to hop over to the chocolate bunnies is a strawberry duck!"

"Not strawberry, Larry, chocolate! It's a chocolate factory!"

"I know that, Bob. I work here!"

Rrrrrrummmm! Chink! Boink! Bop! Dubba, dubba, dubba, dubba. Schlopp! Splat! Dink!

"I'm getting dizzy watching these bunnies going around this conveyor belt!"

Rrrrrrummmm! Chink! Boink! Bop! Dubba, dubba, dubba, dubba. Schlopp! Splat! Dink!

"Then eat one, Bob! They're delicious!"

"I'm trying to read my Bible, but…"

Rrrrrrrummmm! Chink! Boink! Bop! Dubba, dubba, dubba, dubba. Schlopp! Splat! Dink!

"How can you read at a time like this, Bob! We're supposed to be looking for the next clue!"

"I am looking, Larry. How can you eat at a time like this?"

KA CHINK!

"I ate my way to the next clue in Matthew 22: 37–39!"

Rrrrrrrummmm! Chink! Boink! Bop! Dubba, dubba, dubba, dubba. Schlopp! Splat! Dink!

"I wouldn't know… I think I might be sick…"

"Snap out of it, Bob! We've got more important things to do! I've discovered the next clue. **WHOEVER** wants to know the answer along with me will need to read our next issue in the *VeggieConnections News*!"

"Okay, Larry, I'm coming."

"Good job, Bob. That's definitely showing you're willing to do what God wants!"

What are the things that God wants me to do?

"'Love the Lord your God with all your heart and with all your soul and with all your mind.' This is the first and greatest commandment. And the second is like it: 'Love your neighbor as yourself.'" Matthew 22:37–39

Bob and Larry have reported some very helpful news in this edition of the VeggieConnections News.

When Jesus was on earth, he taught us all about God. Jesus wanted everyone to know how much God loves us and how to live godly lives.

When we come to understand who God is and accept his Son, Jesus, and all the love they offer, our heart fills with love, too! So we want to please God and live a life that shows that we are a part of his family. That's why Jesus taught what God wants us to do as members of that family.

God wants us to love him as much as we can possibly love anyone! Not just because that's how much God loves us—but its our way to say thank you. We are a part of his family, and there is nothing more important!

Second, Jesus told us to love others just as much as we love ourselves. God wants us to think about how we would want other people to treat us. God wants us to put ourselves in the shoes of others. And God wants our hearts to burst with love for all the other people he created.

When we do those two things, that is what God wants!

How can I be happy?

Get your climbing boots on as you head over to Madame Blueberry's Tree House with Bob and Larry. That's where you'll find the answer to this question and the next clue:

Clue #9

I can be happy by trusting in God's _____, Jesus.

51

♪♪ "When you're happy and you know it, clap your hands! When you're happy and you know it, clap your hands! When you're…" ♪♪

"I don't have any hands, Larry."

"Oh. Then I guess you're off the hook."

"What are you looking in the Stuff-Mart catalog for?"

"I'm trying to find the next clue, Bob."

"Larry, haven't you figured out where to find the clues to questions about God?"

"I have a feeling you're going to tell me."

"Every clue has been right here in the Bible. That's because the Bible is God's Word. We learned that right from the start!"

"Does that mean you knew where to find all the answers, Bob?"

"I had a lot to learn, too, Larry. And it sure was fun to visit all those places. But the answers to our questions about God are right here in the Bible."

"I hope we helped the kids find out some answers, too, Bob!"

"That's what *VeggieTales* is all about, Larry—helping kids understand that God made them special…"

"And he loves them very much! Hey, Bob, looking in the Bible is a great way to find answers about God! Our next clue is from Psalm 16:11."

"It reminds me how happy I feel knowing what God's **SON** did for us, which is the answer to Clue #9!"

How can I be happy?

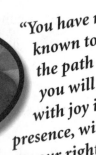

"You have made known to me the path of life; you will fill me with joy in your presence, with eternal pleasures at your right hand."
Psalm 16:11

Bob and Larry report some surprising news. God doesn't promise that we'll always be happy on earth. But don't worry!

God has a path for us to follow, and he is all we need along the way. God loves and cares for us. God is always there with us and wants to hear from us. He'll always listen to our prayers.

God gave us his Son, Jesus, who promises us a life with him forever when we trust in God and believe that Jesus died for our sins.

When we ask Jesus into our life, we are filled with joy—always! Joy comes from connecting to God on the inside. It comes from knowing in your heart that you are never alone.

So even though God doesn't promise that we'll always be happy on earth, we can always feel joy when we believe. And we receive the gift of both joy and happiness when we go to heaven to live with God forever!

That's good news filled with joy!

Wanted: All your unused stuff for kids and families everywhere. God provides all of our needs so we can find joy in being content! Go through the house finding stuff to give away. First make classified ads for your family or church family. Then hold a garage sale or give it to a local charity.

How do I know that God loves me?

Hop on over to just one more place with Bob and Larry to find the answer to one last question. At Flibber-o-loo you'll also discover the last clue to the treasure!

Clue #10

God loves us so much, that he sent us his _____ and only Son.

"The last one there gets a pot on his head!"

"The last one there gets a shoe on his head!"

"Pot!"…"Shoe!"…"Pot!"…"Shoe!"…"Pot!"…

"Gee, Bob, these shoes at Flibber-o-loo are kind of stinky. I think the Flibbians need some foot deodorizers."

"Now, Larry, that's not a very nice thing to say."

"I'm sorry, Bob."

"That's okay, Larry. Thankfully, God forgives us when we do or say something wrong."

"I sure am thankful, Bob! I'm also thankful that we don't have to wear shoes! I'm also glad we don't have to clean out all these pots!"

"Hey, Larry? This smelly boot may be worth looking inside of—it has a sock with a message in it. I think it's another clue!"

"That's great, Bob, but we only need to go to **ONE** place to find answers to our questions about God—in the Bible!"

"That's right, Larry, and that's also the answer to clue #10! Can you tell me what the Bible says about God's love?"

"I'm on it…I mean in it…in the Bible, that is. The good news is from John 3:16."

How do I know God loves me?

"For God so loved the world that he gave his one and only Son, that whoever believes in him shall not perish but have eternal life." John 3:16

Bob and Larry's smelly adventure to Flibber-o-loo had one final clue and an answer to how we can know God loves us.

God loves everyone in the entire world so much, that he wants a forever relationship with us. But how can that happen?

God sent his son, Jesus into the world as a gift for everyone! Jesus taught us that there's nothing we can do to get this gift—because it's God's offering of grace and love that comes to us when we connect to God through a relationship with him.

When Jesus died, he took the punishment for all our sins. By doing that, he made us all brand new again! That's so we can live forever in heaven with God. Heaven is a place with no sickness, no death, and nothing bad. It's a place where we can live in love forever with God.

That's how much God loves YOU! That's a good news treasure!

Five-Day Forecast for
Flibber-o-loo

Hi 95° Lo 50°

Every Day!

What if I have more questions about God?

"I hope the kids remember to look in the Bible for the answers to any more questions they have."

"Or they can talk to somebody who already knows and loves God—maybe even the person who gave them this book!"

"Good point, Indiana."

"I thought you didn't want to use code names, Bob?"

"Well, I didn't. But it is kind of exciting! I could be Captain Bob! Or maybe Sherlock Bob! Or how about Under Bob! Or maybe even Wonder Bob!"

"Hey, Bob? It's a little late for that. This book is almost over."

"True, but there is more good news! We've just started looking in the Bible for answers about God! It's filled with a whole bunch more!"

"You bet! The Bible had all the good news clues we needed to find the best treasure in the whole world— God and his Son, Jesus!"

"Besides, why would we want to be anyone other than ourselves?"

"You're right, Larry. God made us special, just the way we are. And I like being Bob the Tomato."

"I like you, too, Bob!"

"Hey, kids! Now it's time to put our clues together to solve the answer to our treasure verse!"

"Are you ready? Just turn the page and fill in the blanks. There's a special message waiting for YOU, just from God!"

PRESS

Fill in the blanks to solve the Clues to Good News!

"For <u>God</u> so <u>loved</u> the <u>world</u>
Page 7   Page 35   Page 11

that <u>He Gave</u> his <u>one</u> and
Page 41   Page 59

only <u>Son</u> that <u>Whoever</u>
Page 53   Page 47

<u>Belives</u>, in <u>Him</u>
Page 17   Page 23

shall not perish but have <u>eternal</u>
Page 29

<u>life</u>." John 3:16
Page 29

Remember, God made you special! And he loves you very much!

64